CONTENTS

ERRO

PLATEAU of LENG

PHANTOM FOREST

POISON SEA

VULCAN MOUNTAINS

LAKE of GOLD

METAL MOON

DIAMOND MINES

MONSTER ZOO

PITS OF NO RETURN

PRISON STRONGHOLDS

SWAMP OF FLAME

SCARLET JUNGLE

PRISON ENERGY DRIVES

SPACE PORT PRISONER INTAKE

CANYON OF GIANTS

ZAK

THE PRISONERS

ZAK NINE

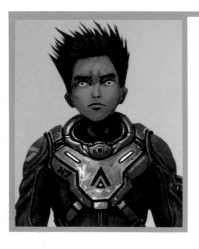

Zak is a boy from Earth. He is a space traveller.

Zak is very brave.

ERRO

Erro is an alien. He is from Planet Quom.

He has fur and a long tail. He has sharp eyes and claws.

Erro is brave too.

THE PRISON PLANET

Zak and Erro are trapped on Alcatraz. It is a prison planet.

They want to escape. Guards are always looking for them.

ERRO'S STORY . . . A DARING RESCUE >>>

Zak was caught by the guards. They took him away. I am free. I followed them. I must find him…

CHAPTER ONE:
THE CAGE

I am in a big stone room room. It is very dark.

Where is Zak?

Sniff, Sniff

I can smell Zak! He is near by.

There is a large cage. Prisoners are inside.

"Zak?" I whisper.

Zak sits up.

"Erro? Is that you?"

Tromp! Tromp!

Footsteps.

Guards are coming. I hide.

The guards point at Zak.

"It is your turn in the arena," they say.

"At last," says Zak.

CHAPTER TWO:
THE BLOODY ARENA

The guards grab Zak. They drag him away.

I follow behind.

We turn a corner. There is a bright light.

I hear a loud sound. It is a roar of many voices.

The guards drag Zak through an archway. There is cheering.

I move closer. I see the arena. It is huge!

Suddenly, there are three aliens behind me. They are Sarkoo from Planet Gulan. They push me forward!

The crowd stares at us. People point and laugh.

"Put this on," says an alien.

He throws me a red robe.

"Start cleaning," the alien says.

I look down at the floor. There are dark red stains.

Blood!

CHAPTER THREE:
GRONTH!

The crowd cheers louder.

A huge creature marches in. It has four strong arms. It has sharp horns.

It is a deadly Gronth!

Zak has to fight the Gronth.

It is a cruel game. He will die!

"Why does the creature not attack us?"
I ask.

"It is trained. It will not attack the
red robes," says an alien. "Now get
cleaning."

CHAPTER FOUR:
CLAWS AND TEETH

The Gronth tries to grab Zak. Zak jumps to the side.

The Gronth raises its hands. It has huge claws. It tries again.

Zak is clever and fast.

But the Gronth is angry and very strong.

CHAPTER FIVE:
RED ROBES

Zak sees me. He does not know how to escape.

I grab one of the extra red robes.

"Over here!" I shout to Zak.

Zak runs towards me.

I bump into a Sarkoo. Then I bump into another one. I am making them angry.

The Sarkoo start to fight each other.
Zak runs closer.

"Put this on, quick!" I tell him.

I throw the red robe. Zak puts it on.
He runs to our group.

The Gronth roars. Zak grabs a rake.
He pretends to be a cleaner too.

The Gronth growls. It cannot find
Zak. The crowd shouts. They want the
Gronth to attack.

A guard prods the Gronth. The beast
turns and roars.

This is our chance. Zak and I run to the
edge of the arena.

"Stop them!" a guard yells.

We throw off our robes. We run through
the archway.

I hear a scream behind me. The Gronth
is attacking the Sarkoo.

The guards are busy with the Gronth.
We will make our escape…